The Dinosaur
with the Noisy SNORE

Russell Punter

Illustrated by Andy Elkerton

Every night, Sid's kept awake
by noises from next door.

He hears a rumbling,
grumbling sound...

One night... "I've had enough," says Sid.

He knocks on Rory's door.

Rory's woken others too.

They cry, "No more! No more!"

Rory looks down. Sid looks up.
"Be quiet, *please*," Sid begs.

"Just buy some ear plugs!" Rory groans.
He shuffles back to bed.

Rory feels bad when they've gone.
Perhaps his friends are right?

He wants to put things right.

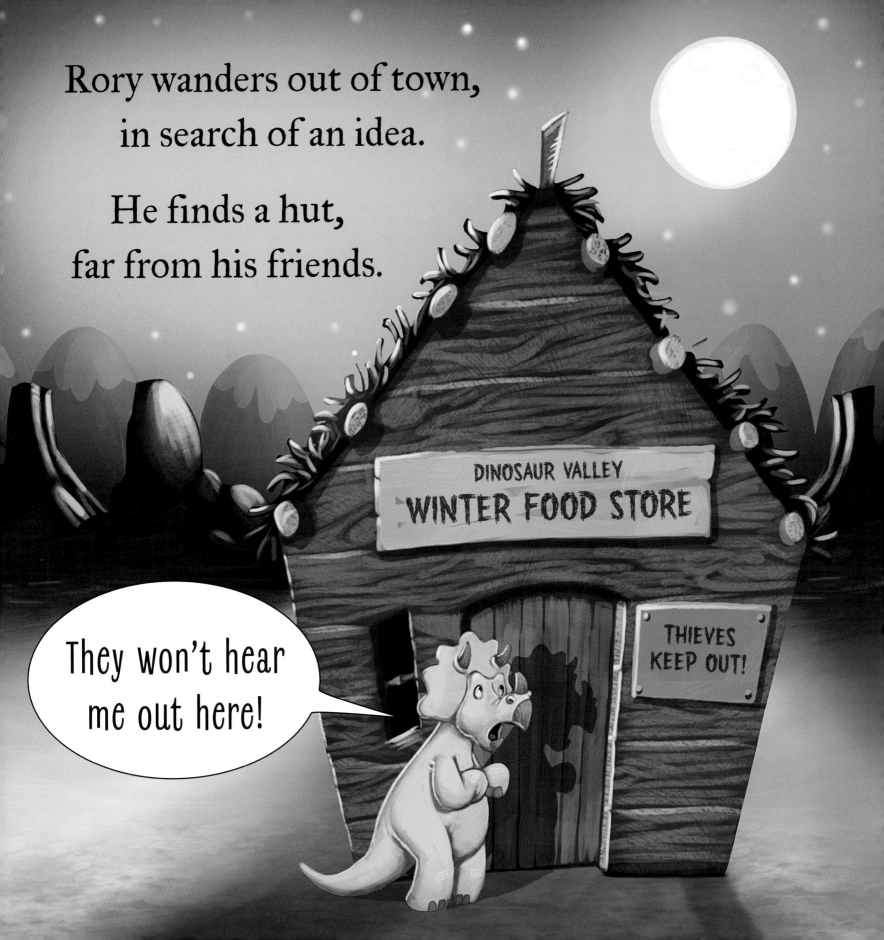

He lumbers in and
falls asleep.

The long, dark
night ticks by.

Three
greedy raptors
wander past.

"Let's steal the
food!" they cry.

They climb inside to take the food.
There's lots to steal, for sure.

Then comes a rumbling, grumbling sound...
a huge, earth-trembling...

"What was that?" one raptor croaks.
"Perhaps a **monster's** near?"

"It sounds **ginormous!**" wails his friend.
"QUICK! Get out of here!"

They all run screaming past Sid's house.
There's panic in their eyes.

Sid wakes up and looks outside.
"What's going on?" he cries.

"We'll leave the food that's in your hut.
Your monster's fierce!" they shout.

"What's that? What monster?"
wonders Sid.

He goes to check it out.

He takes the path down to the hut,
and opens up the door.

There comes a rumbling, grumbling sound...

a loud, familiar

SNORE!

When the new day comes around, Sid gives his friend a shake.

"Oh no," says Rory, "not again! Did I keep you awake?"

"No, you saved our food," says Sid. He tells his chum the story.

Now a new sign's on the hut.

"What monster?"
wonders Rory.

"You're the monster," Sid replies.

Please sleep here every night.

"Your snore will scare off any thieves.

They're sure to get a fright."

"And look – we've bought a bed for you!"

That night, just like before...

Rory falls asleep and gives a rumbling, grumbling, shaking... quaking... HUGE earth-trembling...

Edited by Jenny Tyler and Lesley Sims

This edition first published in 2022 by Usborne Publishing Ltd., Usborne House,
83-85 Saffron Hill, London EC1N 8RT, England. usborne.com
First published in America in 2022, UE.